To April, Connor, and Grayson, you are the greatest joys and blessings of my life.

To my mom and dad, thank you for always believing in me.

To Napoleon, Queenie, and Lois, for planting the seed and for your mentorship and friendship.

To Rod, co-author, shipmate, and brother who helped bring this dream to life.

-Scott

To Kendra, for rescuing me when I was lost at sea.

To Connor, Simon, and Keaton, who make every day my greatest adventure.

And of course Scott, thanks for inviting me to Panera Bread and changing the course of my life.

-Rod

www.mascotbooks.com

The Adventures of Connor the Courageous Cutter: Saving Sarah

For more information, please contact:
Mascot Books
560 Herndon Parkway #120
Herndon, VA 20170
info@mascotbooks.com

Library of Congress Control Number: 2015915350

CPSIA Code: PRT1015A
ISBN-13: 978-1-63177-389-1

The Adventures Of
CONNOR
THE COURAGEOUS
CUTTER
Saving Sarah

Journey with me to a place far away,
Across the seas, and beyond the bays.

Through the big river basins, and just past the capes,
There's a place full of boats of all sizes and shapes.

Come hear their tales, come gather 'round.
And take a voyage with me, to Serendipity Sound!

- Anna the Lighthouse

It was a beautiful morning in Serendipity Sound as Connor the Cutter entered the port.

"You must be the new guy!" a bright red boat exclaimed with a toot of her whistle. "I'm Faith, Faith the Fireboat! What's your name?"

Connor smiled and honked his horn twice, "My name's Connor, Connor the Cutter."

"A cutter, huh? We've never had one of those before. What's a cutter?" Faith asked.

"I'm a fast patrol boat that goes up and down the coast."

"Gotcha. Have you checked in with the big guy yet?"

"The big guy?" Connor asked.

"The Harbor Master," she said. "He's the head honcho around here. You'll hear him through your radio. Is yours tuned to the right frequency?"

"Who's that?" Connor asked while tuning his radio.

"That's Sarah the Schooner. She's a professional racing boat," Faith answered.

"Wow!"

"She's the fastest boat that ever was!" Faith said with a grin. "The pride of Serendipity Sound."

Connor tooted his horn to Sarah, but she kept sailing out to sea.

"Maybe she didn't hear me," Connor said with a frown.

"A lot of the boats around here are uncomfortable with new boats," Faith replied.

"With good reason, too," cried a grumpy voice from the next pier. "If you don't mind, there's old folks trying to sleep around here," coughed Thaddeus the Tugboat.

"Oh, I'm sorry," Connor said quietly. *What if no one likes me here?* Connor thought.

"Never mind him. Thaddeus can be moody, but he means well," Faith smiled. "Just give it some time."

"Good day to you, darlin'," Anna the Lighthouse called down to Sarah. Anna had watched over the sound since before boats lived there.

Sarah looked up, "Good morning, Anna!"

"Have you met the new cutter? He seems like a nice boat!"

"Don't have the time right now. I'm training for next week's race."

"I wouldn't go out there today. There's a bad storm coming. Why don't you take a day off from training?"

All Sarah could think about was winning her next race. "If the weather starts looking bad, I'll head back."

Anna didn't like the idea of a boat on stormy seas and radioed the Harbor Master to let him know Sarah had gone out.

Far out at sea, Sarah zoomed across the waves. Her large sails caught the wind and pushed her faster down the coast. After a few minutes, dark storm clouds covered the sky. *Oh, no!* Sarah thought, *I'll never make it back before the storm hits.*

Using her radio, she called out, "Harbor Master! This is Sarah. I need help!" The waves crashed all around her as the sea swallowed her up. No matter how hard she tried to fight the seas, the storm tossed her about.

A large wave rose high into the sky and crashed down upon her, breaking both of her masts. Sarah cried out, "Somebody heeeeelp!"

Connor, Thaddeus, and Faith were back on their piers, enjoying the afternoon thunderstorm. *As long as I stay here, I'll be safe,* Connor thought.

He heard a voice murmur through his radio. "What was that?"

Faith left her pier at full speed, heading towards the sea.

"Where are you going?" Connor yelled after her.

"Sarah's stranded in the storm! Didn't you hear the Harbor Master's call?" she asked.

"It didn't come in clearly on my radio."

"Someone has to help Sarah! That's what the Harbor Master would want," Faith replied.

"Be safe out there, Faith," said Connor.

"I'll be fine. You have to have a little faith!"

"Why didn't I listen to Anna?" Sarah cried as she was tossed around by the waves. "I wish I were home with all my friends."

Sarah saw a light approaching through the waves. It was Faith!

"Somebody call for a rescue?" asked Faith.

Sarah yelled out, "My—my masts are broken!"

Faith rigged her tow line and tried to pull Sarah through the rough seas, but the big waves kept smashing against them, turning them in all directions.

"We're never going to make it!" cried Sarah. "The waves are too big!

No matter how hard Faith pulled, they kept getting tossed and turned by the sea. They were being swept right towards the rocks. The Harbor Master always warned everyone in the sound to stay away from the rocks.

"Harbor Master, this is Faith the Fireboat," she called out on her radio. "We need help! The seas are too rough!"

"Faith, look for Anna's light," said the Harbor Master. "Let her guide you to safe water."

"I don't see it!" Faith cried out.

"What are we going to do?" asked Sarah.

"The Harbor Master will get us out of this."

Back in port, all the boats were worried about their friends.

"Someone needs to go help Faith and Sarah!" ordered the Harbor Master over the radio.

"I'm not risking it," said Yardly the Yacht. "It's much too dangerous for a yacht."

"Yardly's right," echoed Naomi the News Chopper. "The waves are too big and the winds are too strong for a helicopter! None of us can help them!"

Connor refused to listen to the others. Instead, he cast off his lines and headed out to sea.

Thaddeus the Tugboat awoke from his nap just in time to see Connor leaving. "Where are you going?" Thaddeus called.

"I'm going to help my friends," Connor shouted back as he sped up, "I *can* do this!"

The clouds grew darker, the winds blew harder, and Faith could barely see through the pouring rain. The seas pushed her and Sarah closer and closer to the rocks, when all of a sudden…

"Connor! Over here!" Faith called out.

"Follow me!" he said. "Stay close and I'll cut a path through the waves!"

Faith and Sarah followed so close behind Connor they almost ran into him. Wave by wave, the three of them passed through the surf unharmed.

"Harbor Master, come in," said Connor over the radio.
"I've got Sarah and Faith!"
"Look for my light, Connor," replied Anna over the radio.

Through the dark storm and pouring rain, Connor saw Anna's light beaming across the sky. He turned towards shore as the rain slowly began to fade away.

Soon they were back in the sound, away from the dangerous seas.

"Wow! That was awesome, Connor," Faith exclaimed. "You saved us both!"

Anna looked down, "What's wrong, Sarah?"

"Look at my masts. I'll never race again."

"Oh, Sarah," Anna said. "Just wait until you get back into port. I bet the Harbor Master will make you better than ever."

"I was the fastest schooner on the sea and now I'm nothing but a dinghy." She powered up her little motor and slowly floated into the sound.

"Did I do something wrong?" Connor asked.

"Sometimes," began Anna, "things happen we can't control. Sarah doesn't think she'll ever be able to race again."

"Because she's broken?" asked Faith.

Anna smiled, "If there's one thing I know, it's that there's nothing the Harbor Master loves more than a broken boat."

Connor's eyes grew wide. "Really? Why?"

"The Harbor Master loves fixing boats. That's why he's the Harbor Master. He loves boats more than anything else, but he especially loves a broken boat. I bet Sarah's new masts will be even better than the ones she lost when he's done with her."

Far off in the distance, Sarah sat on a pier by herself, sniffling. Barry the Barge approached her with a crane sitting on his deck.

"Hey dare, Sirrah," he said with his thick accent. "Good ting dat cuttah come save ya, eh?"

"I guess so. I'm just going to go…"

"Go? Go where?" interrupted Barry. "I got dis crane ta put dat mast right dere on ya!"

"What?" Sarah was confused. "Why is there only one mast? I need more to race."

"Don't know. The Harbor Master told me ta bring just the one. Maybe he wants ya ta do more than just racin', eh?" he replied.

Sarah looked at the beautiful new mast and knew the Harbor Master had a bigger plan for her.

Back at the piers, Naomi the News Chopper swooped over Faith and Connor, yelling as all of the other boats cheered, "It's Faith the Fearless and the newest member of our family, Connor the Cutter!"

"Hey, kid!" Thaddeus the Tug Boat yelled. "What did you say your name was?"

Connor looked at the old tug, expecting to be scorned. "Connor the Cutter, sir."

"No, no, no," Thaddeus grumbled. "This is Connor the COURAGEOUS Cutter!"

As his new friends tooted their horns, Connor felt right at home.

From the sound, the Harbor Master could see Anna smiling at the dark storm clouds floating away as Barry the Barge began installing Sarah's new mast.

Connor looked at Faith and said, "The Harbor Master really loves his boats."

ABOUT THE AUTHORS

Photo by Bunny Woodworth

About Scott

A native of McLean, Virginia, Scott McBride became inspired to write children's books while attending graduate school at the University of North Carolina at Chapel Hill. As a husband and father of two boys, he felt called to share fun and exciting faith-based stories with good moral messages to both adults and children. His stories focus on things he truly loves: the Lord, boats, and the sea. He hopes both kids and parents alike find joy and happiness as they share in the adventures that wait for Connor and his friends in Serendipity Sound. Welcome aboard!

About Rod

Rod Thompson currently serves on Active Duty in the US Navy, with fifteen years of honorable service. An award-winning, produced screenwriter of both shorts and features, Rod writes stories that feed the soul and occasionally pass down valuable life lessons. A loving husband and epic father, he currently lives in Virginia with his wife and three sons.

We would like to thank the following Kickstarter donors *who aided in bringing* Connor the Courageous Cutter *and all of his pals to life. We are grateful for your love, faith, and support in this endeavor.*
We could not have done it without you!

Robert McBride
Cha McBride
Virginia McBride
Jackie and Dustin Losey
Kendra Thompson
Robin Thompson
Heather Thompson Szeder
Michelle Thompson Whiting
Richard and Diana Goldsby
Andrew and Ally Minister
Patrick McBride
Chris and Heather Skipper
Leigh and Michael Williams
Dan and Christina Pickles
Ben Kavanagh
Kaitan Gupta
Bob and Kathleen Murphy
John Fitzgerald
Kyle and Konita Wilks
Ed and Jordan Oliver
Meghan and Mike Doherty
Holly Harrison
Malcolm MacGregor
Fred and Beth Gamel
Katie Thurman

Kari Brown
Sara Cahill
Michelle L. Hall
Krystyn Pecora
Karen Kutkiewicz
Carrie and Matt Parrish
Beth Ann Vann
Mike Gawlas
Sara Stires and Chad Redmer
Danny and Felicia Phillips
Phillip Clos
Mark and Lauren Symmes
Geoffrey Voigt
Kate Woods
Bob and Leslie Alger
Michelle Dabroski Artz
Tim Westland
Teri J. Anderson
Jonathan and Allison Cox
Hannah Kawamoto
Mike and Konomi Puffer
Elisha Cook
Rick Leapard
Michael Lawlor
Brent and Latricia Seusy